Skating Sabotage

"Help!" someone shouted in a shrill voice.

Flossie looked around. Amy Cox was waving something red. To Flossie it looked an awful lot like one of her mittens.

"What's the matter, Amy?" demanded Ms. Sloan, the skating teacher.

"When I looked in my bag just now, I found this mitten," Amy said loudly.

Flossie started to say, "It's mine." But before she could get the words out, Amy continued.

"There wasn't anything else in the bag," she said, almost in tears. "Ms. Sloan, my skates are gone. Somebody stole them!"

Books in The New Bobbsey Twins Series

Available from MINSTREL Books

THE NEW

BOBBSEY™

T?W•I•N•S

#21

The Great Skate Mystery

LAURA LEE HOPE
Illustrated by RANDY BERRETT

A MINSTREL® BOOK

PUBLISHED BY POCKET BOOKS

New York   London   Toronto   Sydney   Tokyo   Singapore

A MINSTREL PAPERBACK *ORIGINAL*

A Minstrel Book, published by
POCKET BOOKS, a division of Simon & Schuster Inc.
1230 Avenue of the Americas, New York, NY 10020

Copyright © 1990 by Simon & Schuster Inc.
Cover art copyright © 1990 by Randy Berrett
Produced by Mega-Books of New York, Inc.

ISBN: 0-671-69293-3

First Minstrel Books printing December 1990

10   9   8   7   6   5   4   3   2   1

The NEW BOBBSEY TWINS is a trademark
of Simon & Schuster Inc.

THE BOBBSEY TWINS, A MINSTREL BOOK and colophon
are registered trademarks of Simon & Schuster Inc.

Printed in the U.S.A.

Contents

The
Great Skate
Mystery

1

Warming Up

Flossie Bobbsey hurried into the Lakeport Recreation Center. Only two more days! she thought, pushing open a heavy door. Only two more days until the competition. She gave a little shiver of excitement and walked into the ice skating arena.

"Hi, Carla," Flossie called to a girl with short black hair. Flossie threaded her way through rows of benches until she reached her friend. Then she plopped her skate bag on the floor and sat down. "Are you going to enter the figure-skating competition on Saturday?" she asked.

Carla Turner looked up from double-knotting the laces on her skates. "Sure," she said. "How about you?"

Flossie grinned. "You bet! I've been practicing for weeks. Just think—the winner gets a trophy *and* a whole season of free lessons. I hope I win. I could really use those lessons."

Two more girls arrived and sat down on the bench. Both of them looked to be seven years old—the same age as Flossie.

Flossie recognized one of the girls. Karen Stern had long dark hair, and she'd been at the rink every afternoon. Karen didn't go to Flossie's school, so Flossie didn't know her very well. But she knew Karen was going to be hard to beat. The other girl, who had wavy brown hair, was a stranger.

Flossie bent over to pull on her left skate and tighten the laces. Her blond hair fell in her face. She brushed it away and said, "I wish they'd finish building those new lockers in the dressing room. It'll be so much easier to change and put on our skates at the same time."

"Yeah," said Carla. "And have a place to leave

our stuff while we're out on the ice. They should have kept the old lockers until the new ones were ready."

Karen overheard. "How?" she asked. "The new ones are going where the old ones used to be. You can't have two things in the same place at the same time. Everybody knows that." She sniffed and turned to the other girl. "Right, Amy?"

Amy nodded quickly but didn't say anything.

"Hi. I'm Flossie and this is Carla," Flossie said to the new girl. "Do you like to skate? I love to! But I guess you do, too, or you wouldn't be here. Are you going to be in the competition?"

"I guess so," Amy replied. "I usually skate in the park. But my mother thought I should come here for the competition."

She looked around as if searching for someone. Then she waved. A woman in a big, colorful sweater had just come into the arena. She waved back and circled the rink toward them.

"I forgot my skates," Amy explained. "My mom had to go back for them."

"Hi, Mrs. Cox," Karen said as the woman came near.

"Hello, Karen," Mrs. Cox replied. She didn't even glance at Carla and Flossie.

Mrs. Cox handed Amy a bag made of shiny pink material with a figure skater on the side. Dangling from one of the handles was a name tag. A little white card showed through its plastic window. "Here you are, dear. I'm sorry I can't stay to watch you practice. But remember everything I told you and you'll be fine."

"Sure, Mom," Amy mumbled. She stared down at the floor.

"Flossie?" Carla said, nudging her with her elbow. "Are you ready?"

Flossie gave a final jerk to the bow on her right skate and stood up. "Sure," she said. "Let's hit the ice!"

They circled the rink to warm up. Ms. Sloan, the skating teacher, was at one end, near the big machine that smoothed the ice. She was talking to Ernie, the man who took care of the rink.

Carla came to a stop in front of the teacher,

with Flossie right behind. "Hi, Ms. Sloan," Carla said. Flossie echoed her a second later.

"Hello, Carla, Flossie," the skating teacher replied. "Are you practicing for Saturday? Good." She turned back to Ernie and pointed to a big pile of ice. "Isn't there anything you can do about that silly snowbank?"

Ernie shook his head. "Nope, not before Monday. All the clean-up equipment is locked away until Monday. But the snow won't be in the way. I'll see to that."

"We'll just have to live with it, then." Ms. Sloan nodded to the two girls and skated off.

"It's not really a snowbank, is it, Ernie?" asked Flossie.

"Nah," Ernie said with a grin. "It's just ice that got shaved off by the Zamboni. That's the name of this machine here."

Carla giggled. "It sounds like a fancy dessert. Come on, Floss. I'll race you to the other end."

"Okay," Flossie said. "But then I really need to work on my routine. I want to win those free lessons."

Just at that moment Amy and Karen skated past. They glanced over at Flossie, then looked at each other. Amy whispered something, and Karen laughed.

Flossie felt her cheeks get hot. What were they saying about her?

"Come on," Carla repeated. Flossie pushed Karen and Amy out of her mind and concentrated on her skating.

As she skated, Flossie hummed a song by the TwinTones. She'd chosen it for her routine. Maybe—just maybe—she told herself, the "Twins" would bring her luck.

A little while later she was practicing her arabesque. Balancing on one skate with her other leg extended back, Flossie held her arms out to each side. But she knew she wasn't steady.

Just as she felt herself wobble, she glanced to her left. Karen, in a crouch, was skating backward in her direction.

In another moment they were going to crash!

2

Mystery on Ice

How could Flossie avoid an accident? Karen was heading straight for her!

Flossie straightened up and quickly turned right—too quickly. Karen glided past, not even aware of the close call. But Flossie lost her balance. She could feel her skates sliding out from under her. She waved her arms in big circles like two windmills.

Thump! Flossie flopped down painfully on the ice and began sliding sideways on her bottom. Before she could even think about stopping, she bumped into someone's legs.

Flossie looked up. The legs were Ms. Sloan's. The skating teacher's eyebrows were drawn together. She did not seem very pleased.

"Sorry," Flossie muttered. She tried to get up but flopped down again. Ms. Sloan took her arm and helped her up.

"The first rule of the rink," the skating teacher said, "is to watch where you're going, Flossie. You know that."

"But—" Flossie began. She stopped herself. She couldn't say that it had been Karen's fault, not without sounding like a crybaby. "Yes, Ms. Sloan," she said. "I'll remember."

As Flossie skated off, she passed by Karen and Amy. They looked over at her and whispered again. Flossie clenched her teeth and pretended not to notice.

As the afternoon went on and more skaters showed up, Flossie felt worse and worse. She wasn't really skating badly. But she knew she wasn't skating well, either. Nothing was going quite the way she wanted. Her rhythm was just a little off, and so was her balance.

Finally Flossie took a deep breath and told herself to shape up. She headed for an uncrowded spot on the ice and began spiraling in toward the center. Tighter and tighter. Faster and faster. The figure was supposed to end in a graceful pirouette. Instead, it ended with Flossie flat on her stomach.

"Hey, Flossie, are you okay?" someone asked.

Flossie pushed herself onto her hands and knees and looked up. Lisa Banks, who was in Flossie's class at Lakeport Elementary, was standing over her. She was watching with a worried look.

"Sure, just great," Flossie said. She really meant the opposite. "I love falling down during my routine."

She got to her feet. Ms. Sloan was about twenty feet away, looking over. Then the skating teacher glanced at her watch. Cupping her hands around her mouth, she announced, "Fifteen minutes, everybody. Fifteen minutes till closing."

"Not for me," Flossie muttered to Lisa. "I've had it for today. See you later."

She glided over to the bench, then took off her skates. She bent over again to put on her sneakers. This time her stomach rumbled. It was so loud! Falling down had sure made her hungry. Her stomach rumbled once more.

Flossie looked at the clock on the wall opposite her. Twenty minutes before her mom was going to pick her up. Almost an hour before dinnertime. She didn't know if she could make it!

The snack bar was only a few steps away. On her way in Flossie had noticed a big plate of freshly baked doughnuts. They were her favorite kind—cinnamon and brown sugar.

If only she had bought one before. Now it was too late. Snacks this close to dinner were a no-no. When was the last time she'd had a fresh doughnut? Not for weeks and weeks—maybe even months!

Flossie's stomach growled again. She stood up, picked up her jacket and skate bag, and looked around. No one was paying any attention. Flossie walked quickly to the snack bar and bought a doughnut. But just as she was about to

take a bite, she saw Ronald Jameson—and he was coming her way.

What was Ronald doing there, anyway? He was a buddy of Danny Rugg's, the worst bully she knew. Flossie and her sister and brothers had had more than one run-in with Danny and his gang. The Bobbseys usually came out on top. But that only made Danny, Ronald, and the rest of them even meaner.

Flossie held her doughnut under the counter. It would be just like Ronald to take it. But the older boy walked right past. He didn't even bump into her, step on her toes, or call her names. In fact, *he* looked almost afraid. He was hiding something behind his back, and Flossie caught a glimpse of something red. What was he up to?

Seeing Ronald reminded Flossie about the doughnut. What if her mom came a few minutes early and walked into the rink? Flossie's stomach lurched just a little.

She hid the doughnut in a paper napkin and hurried off to the girls' changing room. No one would see her there. She sat down and took a bite. Before she knew it, the doughnut was gone. So was the empty feeling in the pit of her stomach.

Flossie slipped on her parka, then stopped. Where were her new mittens? She patted both pockets. Empty. Then she reached inside to make sure. The mittens were gone.

Did they fall out of her pocket when she left her parka on the bench? She went back to look.

Only one skater was still on the ice—Karen Stern. Flossie watched her for a few moments. There was no doubt about it. Karen was good. She glided gracefully over the ice, smiling at an imaginary audience. I'm a good skater, too, Flossie said to herself. I bet I can win this contest.

Karen came to the end of her routine. Then she skated over to a bench and started to unlace her skates. Other skaters were sitting there, too, chattering and laughing.

Flossie walked along the benches by the edge of the rink. She tried to spot her mittens, but she didn't see them. Too many legs were in the way.

"Could I have everybody's attention, please?"

Ms. Sloan was near the gate to the rink, holding a microphone. "Tomorrow afternoon, from three-thirty to five, I am scheduling a special practice session for girl under-twelves who are entering the competition. That's three-thirty to five. Please tell your—"

"Ms. Sloan, Ms. Sloan!" someone shouted in a shrill voice. "Help!"

Flossie looked around. Amy Cox was at the other end of the room, waving something red. To Flossie it looked an awful lot like one of her mittens.

As Flossie started toward Amy, Ms. Sloan skated past. "What is it, Amy?" the teacher demanded. "What's the matter?"

"When I looked in my bag just now, I found this mitten," Amy said loudly.

Flossie started to say, "It's mine." But before she could get the words out, Amy continued.

"There wasn't anything else in the bag," she said, almost in tears. "Ms. Sloan, my skates are gone. Somebody stole them!"

3

Mixed-up Music

Everyone gasped. Amy's skates had been stolen!

"Now, let's all stay calm," Ms. Sloan said. "Amy, are you sure your skates were in your bag? When did you see them last?"

"Just a few minutes ago, Ms. Sloan. I took them off and put them in the bag. Then I went over to watch Karen. When I came back just now, the skates were gone. I found this mitten instead."

"That's my mitten," Flossie said loudly. Her heart was pounding. "I lost it this afternoon."

Everyone turned to look at her. "Flossie, do you know how your mitten got into Amy's bag?" Ms. Sloan asked.

"No, I don't," Flossie replied. "I lost the other one, too."

The skating teacher took the red mitten from Amy and handed it to Flossie. "Here's one of them, at any rate," she said. "Do you have any idea what happened to Amy's skates, Flossie?"

"I bet she hid them somewhere," Karen muttered, loud enough to be heard.

Flossie's face reddened. But she looked Ms. Sloan in the eye. "I don't know. I never touched them."

Ms. Sloan took a deep breath. "Well, then. Why don't we all help Amy look for her skates?"

As people started to scatter, Karen looked straight at Flossie. "Boy, I think that's really mean. Imagine taking somebody's skates right before a competition!"

"I didn't—" Flossie started to say, then stopped. If Karen really thought she had stolen Amy's skates, she wouldn't believe her anyway.

Everybody searched the rink. But there was

no sign of the missing skates. "Don't worry, dear. I'm sure they'll turn up," Ms. Sloan said to Amy.

Flossie wasn't so sure. The skates didn't seem to be in the arena. The thief probably took off before Amy even knew they were missing.

Flossie was telling this to Ms. Sloan when Karen came up to them. "I saw you sneaking around before, while the rest of us were still practicing, Flossie. What were you doing?"

Flossie remembered the doughnut and blushed. "None of your business," she told Karen. "I wasn't taking Amy's skates, if that's what you mean."

Ms. Sloan put one hand on Karen's shoulder and the other on Flossie's. "Now, now, girls," she said. "I'm sure nobody's accusing anybody. Why don't we all go home now? Rest up and be ready to do some good skating tomorrow."

Later, at home, Flossie told her brothers and sister what had happened at the skating rink. She left out the doughnut.

Bert, her older brother, shook his head. "That

girl Karen has some nerve. How could she accuse you like that?"

"I agree," said Nan. She was twelve years old and Bert's twin sister. "But what about the mitten? It didn't get into Amy's bag by itself. Somebody put it there—probably the same person who took the skates."

Freddie, who was Flossie's twin brother, spoke up. "Yeah, somebody who was out to get Flossie in trouble. Hey, I know! What if Karen did it? She probably wants to upset Flossie so she can win the competition."

"Don't forget Ronald," Flossie said. "He looked pretty sneaky to me. And I did see him holding something red. He wouldn't care about getting me in trouble."

Nan frowned. "Maybe the thief found your mitten and put it in Amy's bag just to confuse things. Maybe the person didn't know or care whose it was."

"It was a pretty dirty trick either way," said Freddie. "You know what, Floss? I think you need some help with this. What if I come to the rec center with you tomorrow afternoon? I can

21

check around. And maybe we can nail this sneak before anything else happens!"

Ernie was out on the ice, smoothing it with the Zamboni machine, when Flossie and Freddie arrived the next day. The twins sat on the bench with a dozen other skaters waiting for Ernie to finish. Karen was at the other end. She hadn't said hello to Flossie.

I won't let her bother me, Flossie told herself as she put her skates on. Then she took a composition notebook and pen out of her knapsack. She thought for a minute, then began to make notes on her routine.

Freddie looked over her shoulder at the pen. "Why pink?" he asked. "And why does it have a pom-pom on top?"

"Why not?" Flossie said with a laugh. "Nan gave me this pen this morning for good luck. The pom-pom matches the pom-poms on my skates. And here—sniff."

Freddie took the pen and held it near his nose. "Ugh, perfume," he said. "Gross!"

"Not gross. Rose," Flossie replied, taking it

back. She lowered her voice and added, "You see that girl who just came in with her mother? That's Amy."

Amy sat down at the far end of the bench. Her mother was carrying the pink skate bag. She quickly unzipped it and handed Amy a pair of skates.

"Hey, you found your skates," Lisa called out.

Amy's face turned pink. "These are my cousin's old ones," she said in a sullen voice. She pulled one on, then took it off. "It doesn't feel right," she complained to her mother. "It doesn't fit."

"Never mind," her mother said. "I'll put more cotton in the toe when we get home. A champion doesn't let a little thing like this get her down, does she, Amy?"

Mrs. Cox took out a small notebook with spiral wire along the top and flipped it open. "Buy cotton for skates," she said as she wrote. "There." She put the notebook back in her purse.

"Okay, girls," Ms. Sloan announced, gliding over to the bench. "The rink is yours. I have the tape player set up now. Do any of you want to try your routines with music?"

"I do," Karen said quickly. "I've got my cassette right here."

"Amy would like to," her mother said. "Wouldn't you, dear?"

"Who else?" Ms. Sloan asked. Flossie raised her hand. "All right, Flossie," the teacher said. "You can go after Amy."

Ms. Sloan took Karen's cassette and skated over to a table set up by the gate. She popped the cassette into a tape player. The music came on, and Karen began her routine.

"I'm going to look around," Freddie whispered to Flossie. "What about you?"

"I'd better get warmed up before it's my turn," she replied, standing up. "See you later."

Flossie did a few stretches. Then she began to skate at one end of the rink. She wanted to stay as far from Karen as she could get! A couple of minutes later Karen finished her routine and returned to the bench.

"Amy?" Ms. Sloan called. "Your turn. May I have your cassette?"

Amy was still sitting on the bench. She leaned over and rummaged through her bag. "I don't see it," she said after a few moments. "I guess I left it at home."

"No, dear," her mother cut in. "It must be there. I put it in the bag myself."

"Well, it's not here now," Amy answered.

"Never mind," Ms. Sloan said. "You can have your turn later if you find it. Who's next? Flossie?" she called out. "Are you ready?"

Flossie skated over to the bench and grabbed a cassette box from her bag. Then she took the tape to Ms. Sloan. While the teacher was loading the cassette, Flossie moved out to the center of the rink and took a deep breath.

The opening chord sounded. Flossie pushed off, then stopped in confusion. What was going on? The music wasn't the TwinTones.

"That's not my tape," she called to Ms. Sloan.

"It's mine!" Amy shouted. "That's *my* music. Flossie stole my tape!"

4

A Curious Notebook

Flossie dashed back to the table. "May I see the tape?" she asked Ms. Sloan. She looked at the cassette. "This one isn't mine. Mine has my name and address on it."

"Then why did you have it?" Amy demanded from in back of her.

"It was in my bag," Flossie replied. She felt a little tremble in her ankles. But she stood up straight when she saw Freddie listening by the rail. "It was in its box. I just grabbed the cassette and brought it over. I didn't even look at it."

Karen had joined the little crowd. "Come

on," she said, glaring at Flossie. "How did Amy's tape get in your bag?"

"Somebody must have put it there," Flossie explained. How could she make Karen understand the mix-up wasn't her fault? "Maybe somebody was trying to get me in trouble. And *I* want to know where *my* tape is."

"Look, girls," Ms. Sloan said in a soothing voice. "I don't know how this happened. But we'll straighten it all out. Amy, this is your cassette. Here, and try to take better care of it." She glanced around at the crowd of skaters who had gathered. "This is your special practice time," the teacher reminded them. "Don't waste it." As they moved away, she turned back to Flossie. "Are you sure you don't know anything about this?" she asked quietly.

Flossie felt her eyes fill with tears. "All I know is that somebody took my cassette," she said, blinking rapidly.

Freddie moved closer. Reaching over the rail, he put his arm around his twin. "And we're going to find out who!" he added.

Ms. Sloan studied their faces for a moment, then nodded. "Suppose I help you look for it," she offered. "I'm sure it's around here somewhere."

Before Flossie could answer, Amy's mother came over. She gave Flossie an unfriendly look and turned to the instructor. "May I speak to you for a moment?"

"Certainly," Ms. Sloan said. "Flossie, will you excuse us? I'll be right with you."

Flossie moved away from the two women and faced Freddie. He was shifting impatiently from one foot to the other.

"I can't believe what just happened," she said. "Can you?"

"Uh-uh," Freddie answered. He looked both ways, then added in a softer voice, "Do you know who I saw near your bag a few minutes ago? Karen, that's who! I told you I suspected her. I bet she's the one who switched the tapes."

"But she's Amy's friend," Flossie protested. "Why would she do that?"

"She acts like she's Amy's friend, you mean,"

Freddie replied. "Anyway, she didn't really hurt Amy, did she? You're the one who got in trouble."

Flossie nodded slowly. "I see what you mean. Listen, Freddie. I need my tape for the competition tomorrow. Will you help me look for it?"

"Sure," said Freddie. "Let's check your bag again. Things have a funny way of turning up around here. Then I'm going to ask Karen some questions."

A minute later Freddie straightened up from looking in the bag. He was holding something up for Flossie to see. "Is this your tape?"

Flossie grabbed the box, opened it, and checked the label on the cassette. "It sure is," she said. "Where did you find it?"

"Shoved down under everything," he replied. "So the tapes weren't really switched after all. Yours was hidden, and Amy's was put on top. That way you couldn't miss it. Very tricky."

"Oh, Flossie, I see you found your cassette," Ms. Sloan said, skating away from Mrs. Cox. "Good. I was sure it would turn up. Would you like to practice your routine now?"

With a wave to Freddie, Flossie returned to the center of the ice. When the music came on, she began her routine.

Freddie watched his twin sister skate for a while. He tapped his foot in time to the music. She's not too bad, he had to admit to himself.

Then Freddie decided it was time for some serious detective work. Karen was still out on the ice, but he knew which bag was hers. It was made of blue denim and was just a few feet away, next to the bench. Why shouldn't he take a look at it?

Freddie walked casually down the aisle. He sat down, his feet next to Karen's bag. After looking around first, Freddie bent over to tie his shoelace. A moment later he straightened up, shaking his head. The zipper on the bag was closed.

He could imagine glancing into an open bag. But unzipping one that was shut? No way!

Then Freddie noticed a spiral notebook on the floor. It was half hidden by Karen's bag. Could it be hers? It might contain valuable clues!

Freddie bent over to tie his other shoelace. He grabbed the notebook and hid it in the sleeve of

his jacket. Then he moved a few feet down the bench and opened the book.

Karen's name was in the corner of the first page, written in purple ink. On the second page was a list of skating exercises and figures. A couple of pages later was a list of girls, with purple stars next to each name.

Freddie ran his finger down the list until he found Flossie's name. She was one of the few who rated four stars. He laughed when he saw that Karen had given herself five.

Suddenly the notebook was snatched out of his hands.

"What are you doing with that notebook?" Karen demanded. "That's my private, personal property!"

"Uh—" Freddie tried to think of an answer. What could he say? He'd been caught red-handed.

"Ms. Sloan, Ms. Sloan!" Karen called.

Ms. Sloan skated over. "Yes, what's the matter now?"

Karen pointed the notebook at Freddie. "Flossie's brother went into my bag. He took my private diary. I caught him reading it just now."

"I did not!" Freddie said indignantly. "It was on the ground. I was just looking at it to see whose it was."

"You were reading it! I saw you!"

Flossie slid to a stop near Freddie. "You leave my brother alone!" she yelled, glaring at Karen.

"Hold it!" Ms. Sloan shouted, holding her arms up in the air. "Now," she continued once everyone was silent. "Freddie, were you reading Karen's diary?"

"I was looking at it," he admitted. "But I didn't take it out of her bag. I found it on the floor. I just looked inside to see whose it was."

"But you knew it wasn't yours, didn't you, Freddie?" Ms. Sloan said. "Even before opening it? You shouldn't have read it. It's not polite to read other people's diaries."

Freddie, stung, said, "Do you think it's polite to plant a tape in my sister's bag so she'll get in trouble?"

Ms. Sloan's face turned pink. "This practice session is over!" she announced to all the skaters.

"Now, you listen to me, Freddie Bobbsey," she said in a lower voice. "And, Flossie, this goes for you, too. I don't want any more trouble."

"But—" Flossie began.

"Do you understand?" Ms. Sloan continued. "I don't know who did what, but it had better stop right now. If it doesn't, I may have to take drastic steps."

5

The Pink Ink Problem

Flossie barely said one word at dinner that evening.

Afterward, all the twins cleared the table and washed the dishes. Then they went into the living room to talk over everything that had happened at the rec center.

Nan sat down on the rug in front of the fireplace. "The most important thing," she said, hugging her knees, "is to make sure there aren't any more dirty tricks."

Bert looked up from poking the fire. "Right.

Flossie can't skate her best if she's worried about what might happen next."

Flossie was sitting cross-legged on the window seat. "It's not just that," she said. "It's the way everybody thinks I did all those terrible things. You don't know the looks I've gotten. I feel like hiding in a corner."

Freddie, curled up in the big armchair, sat up suddenly. "Okay. We stop the dirty tricks. But how?"

"Do you have one last practice session tomorrow morning?" Nan asked Flossie.

"A-a-ah-choo!" Flossie sneezed. She reached in her back pocket and found a tissue just before she sneezed again. "Oh, great. A cold," she said, sniffling. "That's all I need!"

Then, looking at Nan, she added, "Practice Saturday morning? Yes. I'm pretty sure it's from eleven to twelve. I've got it written down."

"Okay," Nan said. "Why don't we all go with you and keep our eyes open? We might not find out who's behind all the trouble. But we just may stop any more tricks."

She looked at Bert, then at Freddie. They both nodded.

"That'd be great," Flossie said. "But I hope it's okay with Ms. Sloan. She wasn't super happy about Freddie watching today."

"We'll tell her we're there to give you moral support," Nan replied. "After all, it's true."

The big clock in the hallway chimed eight o'clock. Flossie slipped off the window seat and stood up. "I want to wash my hair before bedtime," she announced. "And thanks, guys. I feel a lot better now."

The next morning Flossie sat at the breakfast table, going over her practice notes. Every few minutes she glanced at her watch. Then she looked at the clock, in case her watch had stopped. Why was time passing so slowly?

Mrs. Bobbsey passed through on her way to the garage. "I have some shopping to do," she said, jangling her car keys. "Do you need a lift to the skating rink this morning?"

"No, thanks, Mom," Flossie replied. "We'll ride our bikes over."

"You'll be home for lunch, won't you? You shouldn't load up on junk food before the meet."

Flossie remembered the doughnut and sighed. "Oh, sure," she said. "We'll be back right after practice."

A little later Freddie came in. Flossie looked at her watch once more. "Do you think Nan and Bert are ready?" she asked. "It's almost time to go."

Freddie sighed loudly and rolled his eyes. Why were girls always in such a rush?

"They'll be ready in a minute," he said. "How about you? Do you have all your stuff together?"

Flossie peered into her bag. "Skates, tissues, nose spray, cassette, notebook . . . Uh-oh, where's my pen? The one Nan gave me."

"You mean the smelly pink one?" asked Freddie.

Flossie ignored him. "I hope I haven't lost it already. No, here it is. That's everything."

"What about your costume? Don't you need it?"

Flossie shook her head. "I'm saving it for the competition. I can practice in leggings and a sweater. Now, where are those two?"

"Here we are," Bert said from the doorway.

Nan hustled the younger twins out the door. Fifteen minutes later the Bobbseys pulled up to the rec center. They were parking their bikes in the rack near the entrance when Bert suddenly yelled, "Hey!"

"What's wrong?" Flossie demanded.

"I just spotted Ronald Jameson," he replied. "He saw us and ducked back around the corner. What's he doing here?"

Leaving his bike, Bert ran to the corner of the building. Then he came back, shaking his head. "No good," he reported. "But I'm sure I saw him. I wish I knew what he's up to."

Inside, they found the skaters grouped around Ms. Sloan. She nodded to Flossie. "I was just making an announcement," she said. "From now on everyone should leave all personal belongings by the announcer's table. I hope this will prevent any more unfortunate incidents."

I hope so, too, thought Flossie. She glanced

over at the table. It was set up on the walkway, right next to the rink, so skaters could easily reach it.

Flossie put on her skates and left her bag by the table with everyone else's. Then she went out onto the ice to warm up. She was skating really well.

Then Flossie heard a shout. It was Amy. "Mom! Ms. Sloan! Look what was in my bag!"

Everyone hurried to the announcer's table. Amy was waving a piece of paper in the air. Ms. Sloan took it from her. " 'Quit now or you will be sorry,' " she read out loud.

"Threats!" Mrs. Cox said in a booming voice. "This is disgraceful. Ms. Sloan! You must do something, right now!"

Karen pushed to the front of the crowd and looked at the note. "It's in pink ink," she said loudly. "And yesterday I saw Flossie Bobbsey using a pink pen!"

6

Who Wrote the Note?

Everyone turned to look at Flossie. "Just because the note is written in pink ink doesn't mean *I* wrote it. Lots of people have pink pens," she declared. "Ms. Sloan? Does the ink smell like roses?"

The skating teacher looked surprised but raised the note to her nose. "No, it doesn't," she replied. "It doesn't smell at all."

"There!" Flossie said. "The ink in *my* pink pen smells like roses."

"Maybe the smell faded," said Karen. She

pointed her finger at Flossie. "She's the one who wrote it. I just know she is!"

"Hey, Karen," Freddie said. He'd been leaning on the rail, with Nan and Bert, looking at everyone closely. "What's that pink mark on your sleeve? If you ask me, it looks an awful lot like ink!"

Karen jerked her hand back as if she had just touched something hot. Then she stared at the pink mark on the sleeve of her white turtleneck. Her face turned brick red.

"Er, it *is* ink," she said. "I was writing in my diary, and my hand slipped."

"I saw your diary yesterday," Freddie replied. "Remember? It was all in purple."

Karen looked at him with narrowed eyes. "I switched pens," she said. "So what?"

"You just told everybody that my sister wrote that threatening note—just because she has a pink pen," said Freddie. "Now it turns out *you* have a pink pen. What could that mean?"

"Yes, but—" Karen said, and stammered into silence.

Ms. Sloan raised her voice. "I don't think

accusing each other is going to accomplish anything. Why, I even use a pink pen myself."

Nan stepped forward. "Ms. Sloan, could I take a look at the note?"

"Why, certainly, Nan," the skating teacher said. "Are you going to do some detecting for us?"

Nan gave her a quick smile. Then she carefully studied the note. The paper was small, with faint blue lines. The upper edge was cut straight across but the lower corners were rounded.

"The handwriting is pretty distinctive," she said. "It certainly doesn't look like Flossie's."

"I bet she disguised it," Karen answered back.

"That note belongs to me," Amy said suddenly. She reached over and snatched it from Nan's hand. "You're just trying to make it look like Flossie didn't write it."

"I don't think she did," Nan said. "But the handwriting could be important."

"I think you should let *me* keep the note, Amy," said Ms. Sloan. She held out her hand. Amy pouted for a moment, then gave the note to her. "Now," Ms. Sloan continued, "let's all

forget about this nonsense. We should concentrate on what's important—skating. We're wasting valuable practice time."

"Yes, Ms. Sloan," the girls replied. One by one, they returned to the ice.

"Aren't you going to do anything, Ms. Sloan?" Amy's mother demanded. "My daughter is being picked on!"

"I'm doing what I can, Mrs. Cox," replied Ms. Sloan. "I'm a skating instructor, not a detective. Will you excuse me for a moment?"

Bert, Freddie, and Nan were standing together a few feet away. Ms. Sloan walked over to them. "I could ask you to leave," she told them. "The rink isn't open to the public during practice times. But I hope you'll help me. I've got to put a stop to all this. It's upsetting everybody."

Freddie scowled. "Flossie isn't—" he began.

Ms. Sloan held up her hand. "I'm not accusing anyone," she said. "But I'm not ruling anyone out, either. I simply want this trouble stopped."

"We'll do what we can, Ms. Sloan," Nan

promised. She looked at Bert and Freddie. "I think we ought to ask around—talk to people. Somebody may have noticed something."

"I was sitting right there, putting on my skates, when Amy found the note," said Lisa Banks, pointing to a bench. "I nearly fell off the bench when she started yelling."

"Did you see anybody near her bag before that?" Bert asked.

Lisa frowned in concentration. "I didn't notice," she said. "I was busy lacing up."

"Think," Bert urged. "Did you talk to anybody? Say hi? Anything like that?"

"Well, sure. I mean, people were around."

"Like who?"

"Oh . . . Karen, Flossie, Carla. And Amy, of course."

"Of course," Bert said.

"But that wasn't the only time Amy looked in her bag," Lisa said.

Bert wrinkled his forehead. "You mean Amy looked in her bag another time? Was it before she found the note?"

"Sure, a couple of minutes before. Why?"

"Don't you see?" said Bert. He was so excited he was practically jumping up and down. "The note must have been put in Amy's bag between the two times she looked inside. So anyone who was around during those few minutes could have done it. Anyone!"

Flossie moved her arms and lifted one leg in toward her body. She felt her spin get faster and faster. Then, as she began to slow down, Flossie held out her arms, skating out of the spin in a perfect arabesque. She couldn't help grinning like crazy.

The practice session would have been great, Flossie thought, if it wasn't for her runny nose. Twice she had to go back to her bag for more tissues. The second time Ms. Sloan noticed and gave her a funny look. Why? Didn't she think skaters ever got colds?

"Five minutes," Ms. Sloan called.

Flossie groaned as she headed off the ice. She didn't feel ready for the competition that afternoon. There were still three or four moves in her routine she wanted to polish. But what could she do?

"Nice skating, Floss!" called Nan from the sidelines. Flossie grinned at her sister. But her smile froze in place a second later as a scream split the air. What now? Flossie joined the others hurrying toward the announcer's table.

Amy was standing at the table, holding up her skating costume. The skirt had been cut to ribbons.

Flossie couldn't believe it. Who would do such a thing?

"Ms. Sloan, look!" Karen said urgently. She held up a pair of scissors. "I just found these on the floor. They were right next to Flossie's skate bag!"

7

Cooking Up a Plan

Flossie took a deep breath. "I've never seen those scissors before in my life," she said loudly. Nan, Bert, and Freddie came through the crowd to stand behind her. Flossie felt a little better.

"They were next to your bag," Karen repeated.

"How do we know that?" Flossie said, glaring at her accuser. "Maybe *you* pulled them out of your pocket!"

"Flossie, Karen. Please!" said Ms. Sloan.

"I don't care about the scissors!" Amy cried.

"Look at my costume. It's ruined! Now I'll *have* to drop out of the competition!"

Mrs. Cox hurried over from the snack bar. Putting her arm around Amy, she said, "Don't worry, dear. We'll find you another one."

Amy began to sob. Her mother turned to look at Ms. Sloan. "You promised to stop this terrible trouble, and you haven't. It's only gotten worse. I see no choice but to take this up with the authorities."

"I still believe we can handle this ourselves," replied Ms. Sloan.

"What about the scissors?" Karen demanded. "I found them just where I said."

"Flossie?" Ms. Sloan said, looking at her.

"I told you. I never saw them before," Flossie insisted.

"But you did come over to the table a couple of times during practice. Didn't you?" Ms. Sloan asked.

"I needed to get a tissue."

Flossie glanced around the little circle. Carla and Lisa wouldn't meet her eyes. Ms. Sloan looked sad. Amy was still upset. As for Karen,

Flossie caught just a trace of a smile on her face. The smile faded when Karen noticed Flossie looking at her.

"Flossie's had the sniffles since yesterday," explained Freddie. "Anyone could have dropped those scissors on the floor."

Nobody seemed to believe him. Flossie felt her lower lip start to tremble.

"You all think I did it. Don't you?" she asked, her blue eyes filling with tears. "Well, I didn't. But I'm not going to stay around here, anyway. You can have your old competition! I don't care if I never ice skate again!"

"Flossie, wait," Ms. Sloan said. "Please!"

But Flossie grabbed her bag and rushed to a bench. All she wanted to do was change into her shoes and leave the rink. Through her tears she saw Nan, Bert, and Freddie running around the edge of the rink to join her.

Flossie sniffed and took a deep breath, blinking back her tears. At least they believed her!

Half an hour later the Bobbseys were sitting in their kitchen, eating lunch.

"I don't think you should quit," Freddie said. He took half a tuna sandwich from the tray in the middle of the table. "If you do, people will really believe that you pulled those dirty tricks."

"They do already," Flossie replied. "That's why I ran away. Everyone just kept staring at me!"

Bert shook his head. "Most of them don't know what to think," he said. "That's why they looked at you like that. But the best way to prove you didn't do anything is to find out who did."

"And we can't do that unless we go back to the rec center," added Nan.

"I guess you're right," Flossie said slowly. "And I guess I really do want to be in the competition. But I know I won't skate well. I won't be able to concentrate. I'll be too busy wondering who's doing these things—and why."

"Who and why," Bert repeated. "Well, I still think Ronald Jameson has something to do with it. Why else would he be sneaking around the ice skating rink?"

"Nobody's seen him near the bags, though,"

Nan pointed out. "Besides, why would he do all that stuff?"

Bert shrugged. "I don't know. Maybe he just wants to make trouble. Or maybe he wants to upset Amy and Floss so that one of the other girls wins. One of them is probably helping him. That's why we haven't seen him at the scene of the crime."

"And don't forget," added Flossie, "I saw him hiding something red. It could have been my mittens!"

"Hmm," said Nan. She didn't look convinced.

"Here's what I think," Freddie said. "Who are the dirty tricks aimed at? Amy. And all those fake clues? They point to Flossie. And who's sure to win if they drop out of the competition? Karen, that's who! And don't forget that pink ink on her sleeve. That's evidence!"

"Hmm," Nan said again. "Could be, but I just thought of something. Flossie, is Amy a good skater? Could she beat you and Karen?"

"I don't know," Flossie said. "I only met her the other day. I've never actually seen her routine. But from the way her mom talks, she must be a champion."

Mrs. Bobbsey entered the kitchen in time to hear that. She reached over and ruffled Flossie's blond curls.

"Speaking as a mom," she said, "I think *you're* a champion—even if you don't win the competition. And if it's all right with you, your dad and I would like to watch."

For a moment Flossie's heart sank. What if she messed up? Her mom and dad would see! Then she realized she wanted her family there. She knew that they would always be on her side—no matter what happened.

It was a few minutes before two o'clock when Flossie rode up to the recreation center. Nan, Bert, and Freddie were with her. They were turning their bikes into the driveway when Bert gave a shout. He began to pedal madly.

Flossie watched with her mouth open. What had gotten into Bert? Then, up ahead, she saw Ronald Jameson. He was frozen in place, staring as Bert raced toward him. The skate bag in

Ronald's hand was partly unzipped. Flossie could see the gray blade guard of a figure skate sticking out.

"He's got Amy's skates!" Flossie exclaimed. "Come on!" She stood up on the pedals to get more power and raced after Bert.

For a few seconds Ronald stared at the four cyclists bearing down on him. Then he turned and sprinted up the sidewalk. He was heading around the corner of the building—and out of sight!

8

Ronald's Secret

Freddie crouched low over the handlebars of his bike. If only he had a ten-speed! Flossie was two lengths in front of him. But he was starting to close the gap. He sensed Nan next to him.

"Yaa-hoo!" he shouted.

Up ahead Ronald Jameson had just vanished around the corner. Bert was a few dozen feet behind him.

The curb was coming up fast. Freddie had just enough time to admire the way Flossie jumped it. Then it was his turn. He pulled up on the handlebars and threw his weight backward, to bring the front wheel up. Then he leaned forward to take the weight off the back. He cleared the curb. But the jolt gave him an ache in his elbows and knees.

"Yaa-hoo!" Freddie shouted once more, wanting to take his mind off the pain. He drew even with Flossie as they neared the corner. They both slowed down as they turned wide, then grabbed for their brakes.

Bert had blocked the sidewalk with his bike and was standing nose to nose with Ronald.

"You leave me alone!" Ronald yelled. "I didn't do anything!"

"Then why did you run away when you saw us?" Bert demanded.

"Why did you chase me?" Ronald retorted.

"Because you're hiding a pair of skates in your bag," said Flossie. "Who do they belong to?"

Ronald scowled. "None of your business, pipsqueak."

"Well, I think they're Amy Cox's," Flossie said. "And I think you stole them."

Ronald gave a nasty laugh. "Oh, yeah?" he said. He tossed the bag on the ground and unzipped it. Then he pulled out a pair of black figure skates. "Do these look like they belong to Amy Whosits?" he demanded.

"Those are boys' skates," Freddie said.

"Right, wiseguy! Anything else?"

"They have red laces," added Flossie. "That must have been what I saw behind his back."

Nan, meanwhile, was looking at the skates with an expression that seemed to say, I get it!

"Ronald," she said, "are you planning to enter the boys' figure-skating competition this afternoon?"

Ronald's face turned pink. "None of your— Well, yeah, I am. So what?"

"And you've been coming to the rink to practice your routine?"

"What's it to you?" he demanded. "But with all you Bobbseys here, I haven't had much of a chance, anyway."

"Look, Ronald," said Bert. "I still don't understand. Why all the sneaking around?"

Ronald looked down at the ground. "I didn't want the guys to find out," he said in a low voice. "They think figure skating is for sissies."

"What do you mean?" said Nan. "It's an Olympic event!"

He looked at her eagerly. "Yeah, I know," he said. "But it's not hockey or speed skating. That's all they like."

"Your friends are just silly," Flossie said.

"It doesn't matter," he replied. "They're my friends. Listen, are you finished with me? I've got to change and warm up."

"Sure," Bert said, moving his bike out of the way. As Ronald walked off, Nan called, "Good luck!"

"You see?" Freddie said. "I told you it had to be Karen."

"You may be right," Bert said. "But now we don't need guesses. We need proof."

"What we really need," corrected Nan, "is to get Flossie inside and ready for the competition. We can work on solving the mystery later."

Five minutes later Flossie was beginning to wish she had stayed outside. Carla and Lisa said hi when they saw her, but they seemed uncomfortable. They hurried off as soon as they could.

Other girls turned their heads and stopped talking when she came near.

Then Ms. Sloan saw her and came over. "Good, Flossie. You decided to stay in the competition." But the skating instructor didn't smile, and she didn't sound as if she meant it.

Flossie gritted her teeth. She had to find out who was behind the tricks. She had to prove she was innocent!

As Flossie approached the dressing room, the door swung open. Karen and Amy were coming out. The two girls saw her but pretended not to. Holding her head high, Flossie walked right past them.

No one else was in the dressing room. Flossie took out her costume and admired it for a minute. It was a rose pink skating outfit with furry white trim. Flossie had bought a matching ribbon to tie up her ponytail. The outfit was brand-new. Flossie had saved it to wear in the competition.

Flossie was getting ready to change into her costume when she noticed Karen's and Amy's bags near her. They were side by side on the floor.

Glancing over her shoulder at the closed door, Flossie edged closer to the bags. She needed proof that Karen was behind all the tricks. Maybe it was right in front of her.

Karen's bag was only half closed. Through the opening Flossie saw something red—a very familiar shade of red. It had to be her other mitten. This could be the proof she needed!

Flossie knelt down and reached into the bag. But the instant her fingertips touched the mitten, the dressing room door banged open.

"I knew it!" Karen shouted. "Ms. Sloan! Ms. Sloan, come quick! We just caught Flossie Bobbsey trying to steal from our bags!"

9

A Cold Clue

"I was *not* stealing," Flossie said. She stared angrily at Karen and Amy.

A little crowd had gathered at the dressing room door. Ms. Sloan pushed her way through and closed the door. "All right, girls, what's the trouble now?"

"We went out to get Amy's new costume from her mom," Karen said. She spoke so quickly, her words tumbled one over the other. "And when we came back, we caught Flossie taking something from my bag."

"Amy? Is that right?" Ms. Sloan asked.

"Yes," Amy replied slowly. "At least . . . Karen was in front of me. I didn't really see. But Flossie was bending over our stuff."

The skating instructor turned. "Flossie?"

"I was *not* stealing," Flossie insisted. Her face was burning. "I saw my other mitten in Karen's bag. That's all. I was starting to get it when they came in. Why don't you ask Karen what my lost mitten is doing in her bag?"

Ms. Sloan took the mitten out of the bag and held it up. "Karen?" she said. "Is this yours?"

"No, Ms. Sloan," Karen replied. "And it wasn't in my bag five minutes ago. I bet Flossie put it there herself."

"I did not!" Flossie exclaimed.

Ms. Sloan looked at her watch. "I can't spend any more time on this," she said. "The junior boys' competition is already behind schedule." She paused and jabbed her fingers through her hair. "Flossie, I'm sorry. I'm pulling you out of today's meet. I'm not accusing you of anything. But there have been too many incidents for me to ignore."

Flossie stared at her, not believing her ears. She glanced at the other two girls. Karen was giving her a look of smug triumph. But Amy looked away with an unhappy expression on her face.

"You're throwing me out?" Flossie demanded. Her face started to crumple, and she felt tears fill her eyes. "I can't skate? But I didn't *do* anything!"

"I'm sorry," Ms. Sloan repeated. "I'm afraid I don't have any choice." She turned and walked quickly to the door. Karen and Amy followed her.

Flossie wanted to run after Ms. Sloan. She wanted to be allowed to skate. But she stopped herself. It wouldn't do any good. And besides, she didn't want to give that hateful Karen Stern any more chances to yell at her.

"Flossie?" A hand was shaking her shoulder. Flossie looked up through a blur of tears and saw Nan's face. "Flossie, what happened?"

Flossie grabbed her sister and began to sob while Nan patted her on the back. After a minute Flossie swallowed and took a deep breath. "I can't skate. Ms. Sloan said so. And all because my mitten was in Karen's bag!"

Nan pulled a tissue from her pocket and handed it to Flossie. "Let's go find Freddie and Bert. You can tell us all about what happened. And don't worry. We'll figure out what to do next."

A few minutes later the boys' under-twelve competition was under way. The Bobbseys were huddled around a table near the snack bar. Flossie had just finished telling them about the events in the dressing room.

"I don't get it," Bert said. "What was your mitten doing in Karen's bag?"

"I know!" Freddie exclaimed. "Karen was going to plant it somewhere. She wanted to frame Flossie—the same way she did with the other mitten."

Bert nodded. "It looks that way. I guess that lets Ronald out. I can't see him sneaking around the girls' dressing room. Besides, I had my eye on him while Flossie was gone."

Nan frowned. "Why would Karen take the mitten and then leave it in plain sight?" she demanded. "Whoever found it would think Karen had taken it. And the mitten was at the top of her bag. Right, Floss?"

"Right," Flossie said. "The bag wasn't closed, either. The mitten was easy to spot."

"Too easy," said Freddie. "I've got it! Karen left it there on purpose. She wanted Flossie to reach into her bag. The whole thing was a trap!"

"And I fell for it," Flossie said bitterly.

"Were Karen and Amy alone in the dressing room when you went in?" asked Nan.

Flossie nodded.

"Then they left, and you were alone in there until they came back. That's when they found you reaching into Karen's bag?"

Flossie nodded again.

"This isn't getting us anywhere," Bert said suddenly. "We need more clues—and fast—if Flossie's going to skate this afternoon."

"Skate," Flossie said. "Hold it! I just thought —where are Amy's skates?"

The others looked at her questioningly. Flossie continued, more and more excited.

"They disappeared from her bag, right? Well, where did they go? Nobody would take the chance of being seen with *two* pairs of skates. The thief must have hid them somewhere in the arena. And we've got to find them!"

Flossie sprang to her feet, but Nan put a hand on her arm. "There are lots of hiding places here," she said. "Do you remember where Amy's bag was when her skates disappeared?"

Flossie closed her eyes and tried to concentrate. "Down at the far end, I think. Near the Zamboni."

"The what?" asked Freddie.

"That thing," Flossie said, pointing to the ice machine. "Next to the big pile of ice shavings."

Freddie chuckled. "It looks like a snowbank," he said. His voice died away. The Bobbseys stared at each other. Then Freddie shouted, "Come on!"

They ran down to the edge of the rink and onto the ice, slipping and sliding in their street shoes. Then they began digging into the ice pile.

Ernie, the maintenance man, noticed and came over to see what they were doing. Once he knew, he started to help.

"Hooray!" Flossie cried. "Look!"

There, sticking out of the ice, was the gray blade protector of a figure skate!

10

The Big Competition

"Well, Amy," Ms. Sloan said a few minutes later. "It looks as if we've found your missing skates." She reached down and pulled them out of the ice pile. "I think we all owe Flossie an apology. Don't you?"

"Why?" demanded Karen. "I bet she put them there herself. How else would she know where to look?"

"She's a good detective. That's how," Freddie said. "And you know what? I think *you* hid them there. Then you put Flossie's mitten in your bag to get her in trouble."

"Ms. Sloan, Ms. Sloan," Karen said loudly. "Tell Freddie Bobbsey to leave me alone!"

"Freddie," Ms. Sloan said in a warning voice.

Amy's mother came over, carrying the pink skate bag. She put it down and took her spiral notebook and pen from her purse. "I'm going to make a record of all this," she said to Ms. Sloan. "And I'd like you to sign it."

Carla moved closer to Flossie. "So who did hide Amy's skates?" she asked.

"The same person who took my mittens, and switched the cassettes, and wrote that threatening note, and ruined Amy's costume," Flossie said. She looked at Karen with narrowed eyes.

Karen's cheeks turned pink. "I don't care what you say," she said to Flossie. "I know I didn't do any of it. So you have to be the one. There isn't anybody else."

Nan was bending over, looking at something. She straightened up and said, "That's not quite true. Ms. Sloan, do you still have that note?"

"Why, yes, I think so," the instructor replied. She pulled it from a small purse she was wearing around her waist. "Why?"

"The paper it's written on looks like it might have been torn from a small spiral notebook, doesn't it?" Nan asked. "It's the right size and shape, anyway."

Ms. Sloan nodded her head. "Yes," she said. "But then it would have a row of little holes down the side. And it doesn't."

"That's true," Nan admitted. "But what if it's from a notebook like Mrs. Cox's? One that has the spiral thing across the top. And what if the person cut off the little holes?"

"That makes sense," Ms. Sloan said, studying the note. "The top edge *is* a little uneven."

"Do you see anything funny about the handwriting?" asked Nan.

After a moment Ms. Sloan replied, "I'm no expert. But the tail of the *y* in *you* and *sorry* curls around in an unusual way."

"Like this?" Nan demanded. Before anyone could move, she reached down and picked up Amy's pink skate bag. "Look," Nan said, showing Ms. Sloan the handwritten name tag.

"Why, yes," Ms. Sloan started to say.

"What are you getting at, young lady," Mrs. Cox demanded.

Nan turned and looked directly at Amy. She looked back with wide, frightened eyes. "Amy?" Nan said. "Do you really want to be in this competition?"

Amy's lower lip started to quiver. She opened her mouth, but no words came out. Then she took a deep breath. "I *hate* contests! I know I'm not good enough to win, and if I lose . . . Well, Mom will never speak to me again."

"Amy!" her mother exclaimed. "What on earth!" Amy ran over, hugged her mother, and started to sob.

"I don't understand," Ms. Sloan said to Nan. "Do you mean that Amy did all those things? She hid her own skates and used her mother's pad to write that threatening note? She took Flossie's mittens and switched cassettes and even ripped up her skating costume? And all because she didn't want to be in the competition?"

"That's right," Nan replied. "I got to wondering about her. If someone else had done all that, the person would have been noticed for sure. But not Amy. Who would pay attention to someone going into her own skate bag?"

Flossie listened to Nan's explanation and nodded. It all made sense—all but one thing. She walked over to Amy, who hugged her mother more tightly.

"Why did you get me in trouble?" Flossie asked. "I never did anything to you. You didn't even know me. Why?"

Amy turned her head and stared down at the floor. "I didn't mean to," she said in a low voice. "I was just trying to confuse people. I didn't know those mittens were yours. I just grabbed them and put one in my bag. I had to get rid of the other one, so I put it in Karen's bag. And anyway, it wasn't me who kept accusing you. It was Karen."

"Now, Amy," her mother said, "don't try to blame other people for what you did."

"No, she's right, Mrs. Cox," Karen said, stepping forward. "I was really mad at Flossie. I thought she was picking on Amy. And every time something happened, it just made me more sure Flossie was behind it."

Karen looked at Flossie. "I'm sorry," she said. "I was wrong, and I hurt your feelings."

"That's all right," Flossie mumbled. But she wasn't quite ready to forgive Karen. Part of her still thought Karen wanted her out of the competition.

"The competition!" Flossie exclaimed. She turned to Ms. Sloan. "I can be in it now, can't I?"

"Of course you can," Ms. Sloan replied. "And I owe you an apology as well."

"Ms. Sloan?" Karen said in a quavering voice. "Are you going to disqualify me?"

"Well . . ."

"Don't!" Flossie exclaimed. "Karen couldn't help it. It *did* look like my fault, after all."

"All right," Ms. Sloan agreed. "But as for Amy . . ."

"Amy is withdrawing from the competition," her mother said. "If only she had told me how she felt . . . But I think we've all learned something from this."

Ms. Sloan nodded slowly. "I certainly hope so." She looked around and added, "Girls, it's time to start warming up. Flossie, you'd better go change. And welcome back."

Flossie was standing still on the ice, ready to start her routine. She saw her parents and Freddie, Nan, and Bert in the audience. Then she looked at the judges. They would rate her on a scale of one to ten. But Flossie didn't care about her score anymore. The important thing was skating.

Flossie held up her arms as the music began. Then she took off. Once around the rink she went. Then she skated backward into her jump. Her arabesques and spins were all perfect. Before she knew it, her routine was over.

Breathless, Flossie skated to the edge of the rink while the audience applauded.

"You were terrific!" Freddie called.

She joined him and the rest of the family on the benches. "I *was* pretty good," Flossie said, grinning.

"You were better than pretty good," her father said. "Freddie's right. You were terrific."

Flossie tossed her head and said, "Well,

okay—I was terrific. But Karen was better. She's going to win."

"That's not fair!" Freddie exclaimed. "Not after the way she acted!"

"It's not what she did *before* that counts," said Flossie. "It's how well she skated. And she skated better than I did."

Flossie sighed and added, "I don't really mind, though. But I would have liked those free lessons."

"Well, dear," her mother said, reaching out to give her a hug. "Your father and I have been talking about that. I think you can count on having skating lessons—whoever wins the competition."

Flossie looked at her mother with shining eyes. "You mean it?" she said. "Wow, thanks! And you know what? I'm going to work really hard. I'll practice every day. And next year I'm going to win that trophy. No matter what!"

THE HARDY BOYS® SERIES By Franklin W. Dixon